THE LOST TREASURE

OF

LEVI BOONE HELM

The Funeral

Jacob pulled at the tie around his neck. He felt like he was choking—there were too many people filling up the small room. Everyone's voices echoed off the marble walls and polished stone floor. Someone was wearing too much perfume, and another woman kept hitting Jacob in the back with her purse. Of course, none of that was what was really bothering Jacob, or making it hard for him to breathe.

The real problem was that Jacob was at his father's funeral.

The coffin in the corner was just for show—there was no body in it. Jacob's father had been cremated, and his ashes were sitting in a black urn in their living room back now. But they were at a funeral home, so of course there had to be a coffin.

The reception room was full of family who Jacob hadn't seen in years. There was an uncle who lived in Vancouver, but the rest of the people were cousins and aunts and uncles of his dad, people Jacob had never met. His mother was doing the rounds, thanking everyone for coming, but Jacob had slipped away. He was hiding behind one big pillar, hoping no one would notice him in the crowd and wondering who all of these people were.

Slipping outside into the hall, Jacob pulled off his tie, undid his top button, and ran a hand through his messy black hair. He stuck his hand in his pocket, where his cell phone sat, and debated whether to pull it out. More than anything, he wanted to call his girlfriend. His mom had said it was okay to invite Emma, but he hadn't known how. What would he say? "Hey, Emma, you know my estranged dad who you've never met? He's dead. Wanna come to the funeral?"

He knew Emma could tell *something* was wrong. He would tell her. He would. Just...not today.

His mom poked her head out from the door he had just closed behind him. Her brown eyes were shadowed and tired, and her perfect bun had lost a few hairs. He hadn't realised how grey her hair was going. It made her look old, not like the mom who had protected and taken care of him all these years. "Jacob? You okay?"

Jacob shrugged, and his mom came out into the hall. She brushed his now-messy hair back into place. Or tried to. It immediately fell back across his forehead.

"You don't have to be okay, you know," she told him.

" I don't know," he said. "People just keep...*talking* about him. Like they knew him. Like I knew him."

"You knew him," his mom said.

Jacob raised his eyebrows at her. "Did I? The guy waltzed into town whenever he felt like it. And we let him, every time! I always thought it would be the time he stayed. And then he goes and gets *shot*? Like, who gets shot in Canada? How did that even happen?"

"That damn treasure hunt," his mother said with a sigh.

"That what?" Jacob asked, shocked.

His mother opened and closed her mouth. "N-nothing," she said. "I should get back inside.

"Mom. What treasure hunt? What are you talking about?" Jacob demanded.

His mother hesitated. She glanced over her shoulder and then back at Jacob. "I told him that he wasn't allowed to talk about it with you. It was my condition...for letting him see you. For letting him come home when he wanted to."

Jacob couldn't believe it. "My dad...hunted treasure? What, like a pirate?" He didn't know whether to laugh or cry. She couldn't mean it.

"Just one treasure. A man named Levi Boone Helm buried millions somewhere in British Columbia. That's part of why we moved to Toronto. Your father promised me a new life, away from his obsession. But then he would find a new clue in some old book, and he would leave again, chasing ghosts..." His mother wiped a hand under one eye as if to brush away a tear, even though she wasn't crying.

"Levi Hoone Helm… Why do I know that name?" Jacob asked.

His mother shrugged. "He was a cannibal in the Wild West. A lot of people know about him."

"If he's that famous, why did Dad think he had a hidden treasure? Wouldn't someone else have found it by now?"

"That's the trouble with treasure," his mother said. "People always think they'll be the one to find it. They want the easy way out. They want to be rich. Real life just…doesn't feel as exciting as that. A wife. A kid. A mortgage. Where's the adventure?" She leaned over and kissed Jacob on the cheek. He was too tall for her to kiss him on the top of his head anymore, and he suddenly felt too tall, too serious, too thoughtful. He wasn't ready to be a grown-up.

"Why didn't you want me to know?" Jacob asked.

"Are you kidding? What seven-year-old doesn't want to hunt for buried treasure? I didn't want you getting caught up in his..." She stopped herself from whatever curse word she had been about to say, and instead said, "stuff. Treasure hunts, Jacob...they promise you everything. Then they take everything instead."

That night, Jacob couldn't sleep. He tossed and turned, thinking about everything he had learned. He had Googled Levi Boone Helm on the ride home, making sure his mom didn't see his screen. The man was famous for murdering people (and, yes, sometimes for eating them, which had gotten him the nickname The Kentucky Cannibal), but there wasn't anything written about a buried treasure. Only one page even mentioned British Columbia, and that was just to say that Helm was there for a month during the gold rush, before going back to the United States.

Jacob gave up after the third article. It went into a whole lot of detail about how the man ate a body "like a hyena," and made Jacob feel pretty sick. He was pretty sure he knew more than he had ever needed to about Levi Boone Helm.

But he couldn't keep thoughts of the treasure—and his father's search for it—out of his brain. And lying in bed that night, trying not to think about it, meant it was all he could think about. The treasure. The cannibal. The man who had missed most of his birthdays and every school concert.

Finally, Jacob got up and went downstairs. He got a glass from the kitchen and filled it with cold water from the tap.

Taking a drink, he wandered through the quiet house. His mom was asleep upstairs, and the night light in the corner made everything into shadows. The living room was full of boxes. His dad's stuff had arrived two days before, shipped over from a storage company where his dad had rented space. Jacob and his mom had spent a few hours going through the boxes, and had decided to leave the rest for later.

James opened a box. Before, it had seemed to be full of strange things: a journal, a compass, a bunch of old letters, a leather belt stuffed full of tools, a large wooden box. Now Jacob pulled out the belt. He ran his fingers over the tools. A set of lock picks, a compass, a small hammer and chisel. Treasure-hunting tools. He put the belt on, walked around to feel the weight. For a second he felt really cool, like Indiana Jones or something.

Then he felt silly.

Silly, and angry. Was that what his dad had given up so much for? To pretend to be the hero in some bad movie? Jacob kicked the cardboard box, and the wooden box inside tumbled out. It fell into a beam of light from outside, and Jacob saw that the box was old, and engraved with pictures. As he bent over to pick it up, he heard a gasp from behind him.

Jacob spun around. There was someone in the room with him!

The person was dressed in black jeans and a dark grey sweater, and had a black ski mask over their face. In the first moment that Jacob looked over they froze; then, realising it was too late and they had been seen, they rushed at Jacob.

Jacob gasped and fell backward, pinwheeling to get away from the person. The attacker pressed the advantage, grabbing Jacob's foot and dragging him close. Jacob kicked out with his other foot, but the attacker blocked the blow with their arm. Jacob used the box he was holding as a weapon, clubbing the attacker's fingers. The person swore— Jacob was fairly sure she was a woman—and scrambled after the box. Jacob wasn't sure if she had been looking for the box the whole time, or if it was just a convenient weapon. Either way, he wasn't going to let her have it!

He dragged the box up over his head, using his height to keep it away, and jumped to his feet. "Who are you?" Jacob asked. "What do you want?"

The woman reached for something at her belt. Jacob's eyes widened in horror. A gun. The woman had a gun!

Jacob had never seen a gun in real life, but he had no doubt what he was looking at. And he had a feeling that if he was still standing in front of her when she pulled it out, he wasn't going to make it to his seventeenth birthday. So Jacob did the only thing he could think to do: he ran for it.

They always left their back door locked, but Jacob could see that it was hanging open. He decided that he had a good chance of losing his attacker if he could get over the fence in the backyard. If he went upstairs, his mom might get shot when she came to see what the noise was. And out the front door, there was nothing but a long, deserted street.

As Jacob made it to the door, a shot rang out. Jacob screamed and ducked, almost falling out the door. It was so much louder than he had ever imagined. He pictured the bullet hitting him, sending him to the ground...but as he stumbled down the steps and felt his arms and legs, he realised the bullet hadn't hit him. He was still alive.

Jacob ran to the back fence, running in zig zags like he had heard you were supposed to. Or was that if you were running from bees?! Jacob couldn't remember. Another shot cracked out, and this time Jacob heard it hit the fence, a foot or two away from where he had been standing. He wanted to be sick. Who was this woman? Why was she shooting at him?

Jacob tossed the box over the fence, then jumped up onto the old plastic chair that was sitting by the fence. He grabbed on and swung himself up and over, catching the chair on the edge of his toe and bringing it up with him. He hit the ground on the other side hard enough to knock all the air out of his lungs, but he was safe.

Mostly.

Another gunshot filled the air. Jacob was torn. He wanted to make sure the woman chased him and left his mother alone—but he also didn't want to get caught.

He decided to make as much noise as he could. "I don't know who you are, lady, but you're a really bad shot!" he screamed. He picked up the box, ran across his neighbour's yard, and jumped over the next fence. "Someone call the police!" he yelled. He could hear the sound of the woman trying to get over the fence behind him. From the sound, she was having some trouble.

Going silent, Jacob grabbed a bicycle behind his neighbour's house, silently apologising for stealing it, and climbed on.

He tucked the box into his shirt, tucked in his shirt, and headed for the road.

He had to get out of here—and figure out what the hell was in this box that was worth killing for.

A Lost Letter

Emma was in her bedroom, playing Crokinole with her younger brother, Max. Instead of the regular pieces, though, the round wooden board was covered with Smarties. Every time one of them got a Smartie into the ground hole in the centre of the board, they got to eat the candy-coated chocolate piece.

Emma was very, very bored. Her parents had taken a working holiday to Los Angeles, and she was stuck babysitting for the entire week.

She was just about to tell Max that it was time to get ready for bed when Emma heard something rattle against her window.

"What was that?" Max asked. He sounded excited. Her brother was obsessed with adventure stories—he probably thought this was just like the beginning of one of his favourite movies.

"I don't know." Emma got up and went over to the window. Then she laughed. "Jacob!" She opened the window, and Jacob climbed inside. He looked winded, and he was holding an old wooden box awkwardly under one arm.

"Hey." He kissed her quickly, and nodded to Max. "Hey buddy. You're up late."

"Mom and Dad are out," Max explained. "And if you tell me I have to leave I'll tell Mom and Dad that Jacob crawled in your window," Max told his sister importantly.

"Brat! Mom and Dad won't care that Jacob came to visit," Emma said.

"At eleven o'clock at night?" Max said, pointing at the clock.

"Why are you here?" Emma asked her boyfriend. "Not that I'm not glad to see you," she added with a smile.

Jacob smiled back, but it was quick and faded fast. He held out the wooden box he was holding for Emma to see. "I think...someone's after this. Or me. But I think it's this."

"What do you mean, after it?" Emma asked, her smile wobbling.

"My dad. Um..." Jacob clenched his jaw for a second, fighting back some strong emotion that Emma couldn't name. "He...died."

"Oh my God. What? Jacob, I'm so sorry." Emma reached out for a hug, but Jacob caught her hand instead, squeezing it.

"He was looking for a hidden treasure," Jacob said. "And I think....maybe whoever killed him is after it, too."

"Someone *killed* him?" Max gasped.

"Yeah. And they broke into my house tonight."

Emma gasped. "Are you okay?! Jacob, we should call the police!"

"Yeah, no, we should, but... I just want to understand what this is, first. If we call the police they'll take it away as evidence." Jacob sat down on the ground, putting the box in front of him. Emma came to look, and Max edged closer, too.

"It's...a puzzle box," Emma said, surprised. There were two small circles on the box, and sixteen small round spheres in different colours of wood. The spheres were in tracks, so they could be moved around the box.

"The treasure belonged to a man named Levi Boone Helm. I don't know if this box is his. But my dad was looking for that treasure, and this was in his stuff."

Max reached out and pushed a few of the spheres, but nothing happened. "How do we unlock it?"

"I don't know. My dad obviously couldn't figure it out. But look. There's a strike plate here," Jacob said, pointing at the lock. A small piece of rough stone was embedded under it, with a piece of metal on top of it.

"If you try to force the lock open, it'll strike...and light whatever is inside on fire," Emma said. She couldn't believe it. What had Jacob gotten her into it?

"That is *so cool!*" Max yelled.

"Hey, look!" Jacob had been exploring the box, and he had found a drawer built into the bottom. Inside, there was an old, yellowed piece of paper. When Jacob carefully pulled it out, Emma could see that it was covered in creases.

"A clue!" Max yelled. "Read it, read it!"

Jacob opened the paper. "It's from him—Levi Boone Helm!" Jacob gasped. He read the letter over silently, quickly, then explained what it said to Emma and Max. "It's to his daughter, Lucy. He tells her that he's found a fortune, but the police are after him. If anything happens to him, he's asked a man named Francis Galt to deliver this box to Lucy. Galt has made three puzzles that only Lucy will be able to solve, and hidden them around Canada. If Boone Helm dies, he wants Lucy and Galt to solve the puzzles…and split the treasure."

"Why not just give the money to Galt?" Emma asked, confused. "Puzzles hidden around the country seems like a lot of work!"

"Maybe he didn't trust Galt to give Lucy the money!" Max said.

"He said Galt made the puzzles, though. That must mean he knew where the treasure was," Emma pointed out.

"Maybe not," Jacob said, thinking it over. "What if the final clue is the location of the buried treasure, and that was in a code Galt couldn't decipher? So Lucy needs Galt to deliver the box, and Galt needs Lucy to decode the final clue. The puzzles keep the police—or any other treasure hunters—from intercepting Galt and getting the location of the puzzle that way."

"Jeez," Emma said. "No wonder no one has found the treasure yet."

"And if my dad never figured out how to open it…how the heck are we going to?" Jacob asked. He and Emma took turns looking at the box, and moving a few of the spheres around, but neither of them could see an obvious answer.

"It looks just like our Crokinole board," Max said.

"And that looks just like a *curling* pitch!" Emma said, excited.

"Curling?" Jacob asked, doubtful. "This thing is like a hundred and fifty years old. Was curling even invented then?"

Emma pulled out her phone and did a quick Google search. "Yeah, it was invented in the sixteenth century, and Scottish immigrants brought it to Canada really early, around 1840."

"I don't think Boone Helm was Scottish," Jacob told her.

"But I bet *Francis Galt* was!" Emma said. "And I know a curling pitch when I see one. Try moving the stones into a winning game." When Jacob gave her a helpless look, she grinned and took the box. "Here, let me. One stone on each side has to be in the house . . . then the winning team gets points if they have the most stones close to their house."

Emma moved the spheres on the box so that one was in the centre of the circle. She arranged all of the matching coloured spheres so they were close by, and then moved the other colours so each one was just a little further away from their own large circle.

There was a click, and the box popped open. None of them moved. Emma couldn't quite believe she had done it.

"It worked? It actually worked?" Jacob gasped.

"What's inside? Is it treasure?" Max asked.

Emma opened the box. Instead was another folded-up piece of paper. She handed it to Jacob, who read it out. "Go to the seat of Queen Victoria's newly considered glory. If you seek knowledge, you will find it in the wisdom of the forest."

"Oh god, a riddle. I hate riddles," Max complained.

"Queen Victoria was Queen of England when Canada became a country," Jacob said. "She chose Ottawa as the capital, right? So maybe that's her new glory?"

"When was the treasure buried?" Max asked.

"I don't know, I couldn't find any information about it when I—" Jacob said, but he was interrupted by Emma.

"1862," she said.

"What? How did you find that?" Jacob asked. He went to look over her shoulder at the Google result she was looking at on her phone.

"I just looked up Levi Boone Helm Canada treasure," she said. "There are all kinds of articles about it.

Jacob rubbed his face with a groan. "I can't believe I didn't think of that."

"So, Ottawa. Where do you go if you're seeking knowledge?"

"The university?" Max guessed. "Or the library?"

"The university didn't get its charter until 1866," Emma said after a quick Google search.

"And the first library was built in 1906," Jacob added, looking at his own phone.

"Wow, no library?" Max asked. "That sucks. Where did people go to read?"

"Hold on!" Jacob said. "There was no *public* library—but there was the Parliamentary Library. And look—the library is the only part of the Parliament Building that survived a huge fire in 1916! If Galt did hide a clue there…it could still be there!" … …

"That's incredible!" Emma hugged Jacob, and they all climbed to their feet. "What now?"

Jacob closed up the box, leaving the clue hidden inside. "I guess…I call the police?"

"What if we go to Ottawa and look for the treasure?" Max suggested.

"Yeah, right," Emma said. "This is serious, Max. Someone attacked Jacob tonight."

"Yeah. And she…had a gun," Jacob admitted.

"A gun!" Emma yelled. "Why didn't you say that? I'm calling the police right now."

"I know, I know, I'm sorry," Jacob said. "I just had to know what the box had in it. And it's only been a few minutes. There's no way she followed me here."

"Are you sure?" Max asked. "Cuz, um…"

He pointed out the window, and Emma and Jacob both rushed to his side. Someone was in the yard—standing next to the bike that Jacob had left, clearly visible, by the side of the house. Before they could duck out of sight, she looked over—and her eyes caught Jacob's.

Jacob swore and slammed the window closed, locking it. "Is the front door locked?" he asked Emma.

She shook her head, terrified. "I always lock it right before we go to bed. What do we do?!"

"I'll go. Hopefully, she'll follow me," Jacob said.

"What if she *doesn't*?" Emma pointed out. "If she thinks we have the box she might not follow you! I'm calling 911." Emma opened the phone app on her cell phone and dialled. But nothing happened. When she looked closer, she saw that her bars were at zero—and even her wifi was down. "My phone!" she gasped.

Jacob checked his, too. He shook his head. It was down, too. "A signal jammer?" he asked.

"Those are *real*?" Max asked.

"Yeah, but they're also illegal!" Emma said.

"I'm pretty sure this woman killed my dad!" Jacob reminded her. "I don't think she's worried about breaking the law. We have to get out of here. Come on!"

He grabbed Max's hand, and the three of them dashed out of the bedroom and down the stairs. They could hear the attacker at the back door, trying to force the lock.

Emma grabbed her purse, and she and Max both stuffed their feet into sandals before bursting out the front door. They took off running, down the block.

"Where to?" Emma asked, looking over her shoulder.

"Where's the nearest police station?" Jacob asked.

"I have no idea! Psychopaths don't chase me through my middle-class suburban neighbourhood very often!" Emma moved Max so that he was between her and Jacob, just in case, and looked over her shoulder again. The woman had just appeared from around the house. "She's there!" Emma screamed.

Jacob considered the box in his hands. Then he turned and threw it behind them.

"You can't!" Max yelled. He started to turn around but Emma grabbed his arm and dragged him forward.

"It'll take her ages to get it open," Jacob promised. "And hopefully, it'll stop her from shooting us!!"

Sure enough, their attacker stopped to pick up the box. Emma, Jacob, and Max turned at the nearest corner. They kept running until poor Max couldn't go one more step; then they stopped to catch their breaths.

"What now?" Emma asked.

"I have to get to Ottawa and find the clue before she does," Jacob said. "This treasure…my dad died trying to find it. I can't just let the woman have it. You take Max and go tell the police what happened. Hopefully, they can catch her before she leaves the city."

"No way—I'm going with you," Emma said.

"Me too!" Max agreed.

"You're not coming," Emma told him. "It's way too dangerous!"

"Staying here is *just* as dangerous," Max pointed out. "She saw all three of us. If she gets the box open, she'll know we're after the treasure. She might grab me to use as leverage, or make her tell her where the treasure is, or anything awful!"

"You're right," Emma told him. She looked over at Jacob. "We have to drop him off with the police before we go."

"No!" Max yelled.

"I don't know if there's time…" Jacob looked back over his shoulder, even though there was nothing to see.

"Good point," Max said. He grinned and took off down the street, running as fast as his tired legs could go.

"Max! Stop it, are you crazy?" Emma screamed. She ran after him. With a groan and a deep breath, Jacob followed.

"We have to get to the bus station before it's too late!" Max yelled over his shoulder. "If you waste time trying to stop me from coming with you, you'll never get there in time!"

"Let's just bring him," Jacob said. "He's right—he's probably safer with us than on his own."

Emma gulped. It seemed crazy to bring him but... "Are you sure?"

"Don't worry," Jacob promised. "We'll take care of him."

Emma nodded and turned her attention back to her brother. But inside, she wasn't at all sure that she was doing the right thing.

The Forest of Knowledge

Jacob shook Emma awake. It was a little after five in the morning, and they had just arrived in Ottawa, Canada's capital city. On one side of the street, an old stone building rose three stories, its arched windows giving it the look of a library or a church. On the other side, a department store with modern red tiles stood next to a bookstore and a Starbucks Express. Everything was closed.

Last night, Jacob had used his emergency credit card to buy them all tickets for an overnight bus. He had sent an email to his mother, telling her what happened and asking her to call the police. Max had slept on the bus, but Emma had only napped, and Jacob hadn't been able to sleep at all. He couldn't believe they were really on the trail of the treasure his father had died trying to find. What would it be like, to hold it in his hands? To do what his father hadn't been able to do?

The Parliament Buildings didn't open until 8:30, so the trio went into Tim Hortons and ordered coffee and doughnuts. They sat and talked strategy, then took turns napping in their booth, out of view of the people serving coffee at the counter.

Finally, just after 8:30, the three of them left the coffee shop. The Parliament Buildings were only a few blocks away. They were four big stone buildings with green copper roofs and a huge green lawn. A giant clock tower was at the centre. The kids went into the building, which was open to the public. They walked through metal detectors, and Emma put her bag through the scanner, and then they were inside. The ceilings were tall and vaulted, and columns and arches lined the long hallway. The floor was polished white stone. Even early in the morning, it was busy, with politicians on their way to work and aides running everywhere.

They walked down the long hall toward the library at the end. Emma nudged Max and pointed at the wall. "Look," she whispered.

She touched a spot on the marble. There were chips in the stone—bullet holes from a terrorist attack a decade ago.

Shivering, they kept walking. Inside the library, all three of them stopped to look around. It was beautiful. The room was a huge circle, with a big white statue of Queen Victoria in the centre of the room. Thousands of flowers, masks, and animals were carved into the white pine panelling. The ceiling rose into a huge dome, and every wall was covered in books. This early in the morning it was mostly empty, though a few librarians moved around, reshelving books.

"How will we find a clue in all of this?" Emma whispered.

"We're looking for the wisdom of the forest," Jacob reminded her.

"A tree? A leaf?" Max asked.

All three of them turned to look at the walls. There were carvings everywhere.

"Oh, God," Emma said. "It's like finding…"

"A tree in a forest," Jacob joked.

"We'd better get started," Emma said. With a sigh, they headed over to the walls and began to look.

After an hour, Max had fallen asleep in a chair at one of the reading tables. Emma and Jacob were still searching the walls, looking for any carvings that stood out. They had looked over about half of the room when Jacob found a carving that looked different. It was of a tree, surrounded by seven leaves. Each leaf had a small carving on it: a fish, a gold nugget, an old musket gun, a bird, a potato, an orca whale, and wheat.

"Emma!" Jacob called as quietly as he could, waving his arms to get her attention. She hurried over to look at what he had found. "It doesn't match any of the carvings," he said. "Everything else is really simple, but these leaves have these symbols in them."

"Look! They're loose," Emma said. She stuck her fingernail under a leaf and, with some effort, managed to get it out. She did the same to the next, and the next.

"Maybe we have to put them in order?" Jacob said.

"But what order? There are seven leaves...that could make a million different combinations."

"Maybe...bird eats fish, orca eats bird, bird is shot by gun..."

"What about the gold?" Emma asked.

"Oh, I thought that was poo," Jacob said, laughing.

"Gross! Would you focus?" she said, shoving him playfully.

They sat down cross-legged on the floor and laid the seven leaves out in front of them. Jacob ran his fingers gently over the carvings. "The last one was a sport. Maybe...hockey teams?"

"Did we have hockey teams yet?"

Jacob took out his phone to check and shook his head. "1909."

"The treasure Levi buried was gold," Emma said, touching that leaf.

"And he buried it in British Columbia—where there was a gold rush!" Jacob said. Excited, he laid out the leaf with the gold nugget. "And what's next to B.C.? Alberta, the province famous for its wheat!" He put that leaf down next.

"There are only seven leaves, though. There are ten provinces and three territories."

"Regions, maybe? Alberta, Saskatchewan, and Manitoba are all prairies. So then we'd be at Ontario next."

"The gun?" Emma suggested. "Ontario and Quebec were always fighting in those days."

"Yes! And then a bird for the East Coast, and fish. And a potato? I don't know, that's a lot for the East Coast." Jacob scratched his head, frowning.

"And what about the orca? That's got to be B.C., right? I went to Victoria once with my mom and there were tons of whale-watching tours. So then where does the gold go?"

"Hold on…" Jacob went back to his phone and Googled the original British territories. He looked up at Emma with a grin. "Guess how many British territories there were before confederation?"

"Seven?" Emma asked hopefully.

"You got it!" Jacob stood up and gathered the leaves. One by one, he put them into the carving. "Orca for Vancouver Island. Gold for B.C., a gun for Ontario and Quebec, or, as it was known then, the territory of Canada. Fish for New Brunswick, a bird for Nova Scotia, and…a potato for Prince Edward Island." As Jacob clicked the last leaf back into place, the trunk of the tree rumbled. After a second, it popped out, revealing a small compartment. Jacob pulled out a folded-up note as Emma clapped her hands, thrilled.

"Another riddle!" he told her.

"Wait, let me wake Max up," Emma said. She hurried over and got her brother while Jacob read the note. When they were back, she asked him, "What does it say?"

"It's not a riddle," Jacob said. "I think it's…a map?"

All three of them clustered around to look at the paper he held. It did look like a map, but covered in little notes. It showed a hill, with a large X on it. There were waves on the left side, with a small boat in them. The notes were scattered and random. "Defender," "the deep," "high above," "~~home~~ new," and "star."

"So it's a building, on a hill, by the water," Max said.

"A place with ships, so probably the ocean, not a lake," Emma pointed out.

"Or the St. Lawrence," Jacob said "Ships go down that river all the time."

"Home is crossed out," Max said, pointing to that. "What does it say above it? New?"

"Not home. But new… Nova Scotia! That's New Scotland, and Galt was Scottish," Jacob said.

"And the water is on the left. Nova Scotia is on the East Coast!" Emma grinned. "So what are some famous landmarks in Nova Scotia?"

"A place on a hill. That defends ships…a lighthouse? The Peggy's Cove lighthouse!" Jacob said.

"That's got to be it!" Emma hugged Jacob and ruffled Max's hair.

"I guess we're on our way to Halifax," Jacob said.

"How? Do you know how much plane tickets to Halifax will cost?" Emma told him. "Your mom would *kill you* if you put that on her card."

"We could take the bus," Max said

"It would take hours," Emma said. She checked her phone again. "Like...fifteen hours."

"If we get the treasure, I can pay her back for the tickets. And then some!" Jacob said.

"But we have the clue now. Whoever that woman is, she won't be able to find the treasure. We can go back home, tell your mom everything, and get her to help us."

"Or she could just get the security footage and read the note over your shoulder," Max said. He pointed up...way up...to where a security camera was clearly pointing right at them. They all looked down at the map...that Jacob was holding perfectly flat, in view of the camera.

Jacob winced and stuffed it in his pocket. "So...Halifax?"

Emma sighed. "Halifax," she agreed.

They took a bus out to the airport, where they were lucky to find a flight from a discount airline leaving at noon. It would get them to Halifax by 2 p.m. and only cost a few hundred dollars each. Since the regular airline was charging $600 for one ticket, Jacob counted himself lucky as he handed over his credit card and hoped his mom would forgive him.

"Why this treasure?" Jacob asked Emma. They were sitting in the airport lounge, eating a quick lunch before their flight.

"What do you mean?" she asked.

"Mom said my dad was obsessed with finding Levi Boone Helm's lost treasure. But there are so many lost treasures in the world. He gave up so much to hunt for this one... I can't help but wonder why. What it meant to him."

"Maybe we'll find out when we find the treasure." She reached for his hand, and he took hers and held it tight.

"I hope so. I never really knew him. I wonder if... I don't know, it's stupid."

"It's not stupid," Emma said. "I get it. You want to know why he wasn't there for you. What made it worth it."

Jacob nodded. He hoped that finding the treasure would help him understand his father. Who he had been...and what he had died for.

Disaster at Peggy's Cove

Emma and Jacob both slept on the short flight to the East Coast. As soon as the trio landed in Halifax, they went to an information desk to find out how to get to Peggy's Cove. It turned out it was only an hour away—but there was no public transportation out to the tourist attraction. They were too young to rent a car, and most taxis wouldn't take the long trip. The information employee helped them call around to tour companies, to see if any were leaving soon. Most of them left in the morning, but they found one that would take them out to the lighthouse, and then cruise back to Halifax Harbour by boat to take in the sunset. Jacob nervously handed over his credit card again, worrying about when he would hit the limit, but it went through.

Half an hour later, they were on a tour bus on their way to Peggy's Cove.

Around four o'clock, the bus drove through the small town of Peggy's Cove and pulled into the lighthouse's busy parking lot. The trio got out and looked around. There were people everywhere—most of them had come by car, but there were a few other tour buses, too. There was a pretty, white-washed old building with an Information Center inside, and then a huge rocky area that people were climbing across to reach the lighthouse. There was a path, too, but Max took off over the rocks. Jacob and Emma followed, laughing.

They reached the lighthouse and took a moment to look at the beautiful view. Atlantic waves crashed against the rock cliff, and the sea stretched out to the horizon.

Seabirds flew above them, and the smell of salt was in the air. It was incredible.

"What now? The map didn't have any clues about what to look for," Emma said.

Jacob looked around. "There—" He pointed at a sign that had information for tourists. "Maybe that can tell us which parts of the lighthouse are original, so we know what to look for."

Max ran ahead to read the sign. By the time Emma and Jacob got there, Max was looking at them in horror. "Guys…"

"What's wrong?" Emma asked.

"The lighthouse was replaced in 1914," Max told them.

"What?! No!" Jacob quickly re-read what Max had just looked over. "Wait! It says the old wooden lighthouse was used as the keeper's dwelling! It should…" He stopped, and took a stumbling step away from the sigh.

"It fell apart during a hurricane in the 50s," Max told Emma. "It's gone."

"But…" Emma looked around, helplessly. "There must be something…"

"The clue is gone," Jacob said. "We came all this way…for nothing."

It was a quiet boat ride back to Halifax. Max fell asleep, and Emma rested her head on Jacob's shoulder. It should have been a romantic ride. The sun was close to setting, and the ocean was a thousand shades of red, yellow, orange, and blue. The breeze over the water was cool but not cold, and Halifax's harbour was full of buildings. Their windows glowed with light, warm and inviting. But Jacob was angry and depressed. He couldn't believe they had come all this way with nothing to show for it.

Jacob took out the map and looked at it again. Why had Galt chosen to hide the clue in a wooden lighthouse? He had no way of knowing that Peggy's Cove would become so popular with tourists.

The tour guide had been droning on for a while. Jacob listened as she said, "And coming up on our right you'll see the Halifax Citadel. This fort was first built in 1749, but the construction you need now was completed in 1856, and was upgraded so that it could defend the harbour as well as land attacks."

Jacob, who was staring down at the map, suddenly let go of Emma's hand. He lifted the map up… "Defender. Stars. Ships. Oh my god, it's the Citadel!" he yelled. A few heads turned their way, and Max woke up, blinking and looking around in confusion.

"What's the Citadel?" Emma asked.

"I couldn't figure out why Galt would hide the clue at the lighthouse. From what we read when we were there, it wasn't a popular or famous attraction. And it was made of wood! He had to know there was a chance it wouldn't be there by the time Lucy was old enough to go and get the treasure. But what if he didn't? We know 'new home' is Nova Scotia. We thought 'defender, the deep, and high above' was the lighthouse. But the Citadel is all of those things, too. It's a fort, built on a hill, that defends from land and sea. And the final clue, 'star!' I thought that meant nighttime, when the lighthouse would be lit. But the Citadel is *shaped like a star.*"

Emma stared at the clues and then up at the Citadel. They could just see it peeking up from the nearby hill. "Jacob—I think you're right!" she said, excited. "This could be it!"

The Citadel closed to the public at five o'clock, but they ran ghost tours in the evening. There was a fancy fish restaurant across the street, so the trio stopped for freshly caught Atlantic lobster while they waited for the tour. As they sat in the restaurant, Max licking butter from his fingers, they poured over maps of the Citadel on their phones.

"The Citadel is huge," Emma said, worried. "We have to narrow down our search before we get in there."

"Look at where he's written defender," Jacob said, showing them the clue again. "It's right outside one of the lines of the X that marks the Citadel. I bet that means it's hidden somewhere along the outside of the fort, where the defenders would have stood," Jacob said.

Emma considered that. She went from map to map, then held one up. "Look—see this path that goes all around the outside of the fort? This map labels it as the musket gallery. That would have been a good place for defenders to stand—and it's on the outside, just like the clue shows."

"That's still a pretty long tunnel," Max said, worried.

"We had to look at every panel on every wall in the library," Jacob reminded him. "We can look over one tunnel."

"Okay. We'll start the tour with everyone else, and then slip away when they head inside," Emma said. The group agreed, and Jacob left to pay their bill.

The Citadel was a huge stone fortress built right into the top of the hill. To reach it, they had to walk across a drawbridge over a large dry moat. Modern safety railings kept them from falling ten feet or so into the empty moat. In front of them was a huge double door with a castle gate that stood open. As they walked over, Emma nudged Jacob and pointed to their left. They could see a section of the musket gallery—wooden stairs led up to the tunnel, and rifle holes were cut out all along the wall. That was where they would have to make their way—and without being spotted.

At the front gate, they waited with the other tourists who were taking the ghost tour. The tour guide met them not long after, dressed in full historical clothes, including a tiny round red hat. He was a friendly man with a big, dramatic voice that carried well. He started out by giving them a little bit of the history of the Fort as they walked through the causeway into the large open area in its centre. "In the late 1940s," he said, "a lot of people in the Halifax business community wanted to tear the fort down and turn it into parking for their businesses. Luckily for us, and the history of this place, they failed to do that. In the 1990s, the city restored the fort back to its 1869 appearance."

"Restored?" Jacob whispered. "Does that mean it's all new?"

They all stared at the guide, nervous now.

The guide continued. "They broke down the walls, adding wiring and waterproofing, and then put them back together—restoring every single stone to its original location. And they must have restored the ghosts back to their places, too, because we have all kinds of local hauntings!"

Max shivered and looked around. "Ghosts?"

"Don't worry," Emma said. "Even if they're real, they won't hurt us. We're not here to ruin their fort. Just take a little something away with us. And if they put all the stones back where they found them…hopefully, Galt's puzzle is still hiding right where he left it."

The guide was still talking. "If you look closely at the walls, you can see coins in the mortar showing the date the wall was rebuilt. Now if you follow me through here, we're going to start our tour in…the dungeons! Prisoners were kept here, and it's…"

The tour followed the guide through the door into the keep: a wide-open parade square. There was a large building right in front of them, and small tunnels called sally ports leading away, back through the main wall toward the musket gallery. As the rest of the group went toward the central building, the trio hung back by the wall. When no one was looking, they slipped through the sally port just to the left of the gate and back to the outside of the wall.

Max was the first one to find the narrow wooden staircase that led up to the musketry gallery. They went through a small door and came out in a pitch-black tunnel. After some fumbling, Emma and Jacob both took out their cell phones and turned on their flashlights. In the blinding white light, they could see that the floor was packed dirt. The walls were made of stone, and the little rifle holes didn't let in much light at all.

Carefully, the three kids started to look over the walls. "Look for carvings, like last time," Jacob said.

"Here's one!" Emma said. Then she shook her head. "It just says Jones 1883."

"Hundred-year-old graffiti!" Max said. "That's cool!"

"Cool," Jacob agreed, "but not what we're looking for." He took a step back to get a better look at the wall. "Hang on...is it my imagination, or are there four different coloured stones in the wall?"

Emma and Max both stood up and looked. The wall was made of mortared stone, uneven enough that small differences in the stones weren't obvious right away. But now that they were looking at it closely, it was clear that a small patch of wall, about ten feet long, had more different kinds of stones than the other sections did.

"I don't see a pattern," Max said.

"Is it making an image?" Jacob asked. "Or maybe a map of where the next clue is?"

"Four different kinds..." Emma said. Quickly, she counted the stones. "These three are a bit lighter than normal, these five are darker. These two have sort of white lines in them, and these six have carved marks. Three, five, two, six. Could it be a combination?"

They all looked around, but there was no combination lock or place to put the numbers in.

"Wait!" Jacob said, excited. "Galt wanted to make sure that Lucy worked with him on the clues. He might have made sure this clue needed two people to unlock. Four numbers, four hands! Emma, try gently pushing on the third and fifth stone." Jacob pointed, and Emma raced over. She had to stretch her arms out, but she could just reach. Jacob went to the other wall and put his hands on the second and sixth stones. As his hand came down on the final stone, a low grinding noise filled the air.

They looked down and saw that one of the stones at the bottom of the wall had sunk a few inches into the wall. It revealed a tiny hole....with a piece of paper inside!

Jacob grabbed the paper. As he let go of the stones, the opening quickly shut, hiding the now-empty hole.

"We did it!" Emma said. She and Max high-fived as Jacob opened the paper and read it over.

He handed it to Emma. "What do you think?" he asked.

"*I* think," a woman's voice said, "that you're going to give that paper to me."

They all turned around at once. A woman was standing in front of them. She was tall, with messy brown hair and thin eyebrows. She was wearing black pants...and a grey sweater...and she was holding a gun, pointed right at Jacob.

"You," he said. It was definitely the same woman who had followed them from Toronto. She had gotten the clue from the cameras after all. He wondered who she was, that she could access cameras at the Parliament Buildings.

"Me. And that's my clue." She pointed the gun at Emma.

Jacob stepped between them, his hands outstretched to show that he wasn't a threat. "Who are you? Why are you doing this?" Jacob asked.

The woman's face twisted into a hard, ugly shape. "This treasure is my birthright. Your dad tried to steal it—to keep it for himself. Now you're going to hand it over."

"And then what? You kill us?" Jacob asked.

"I don't want to fire this gun if I don't have to," the woman said. "It'll bring a lot of attention. Your girlfriend gives me the clue, and I let you all walk away."

"You didn't let my dad walk away." Jacob clenched his hand into a fist. Emma put a hand on his arm. She was scared, but she nodded. She trusted him to do whatever he needed to do.

"He wasn't reasonable," the woman said. "Are you going to be?"

"Give it to her," Jacob said.

"What? Are you sure?" Emma asked him quietly.

"It's just money. It isn't worth getting shot over," Jacob said. He squeezed her hand, as if to say… trust me. Emma nodded. Motioning Max to stay behind Jacob, just in case, she edged in front of him and held out the paper, staying as far back from the woman as she could. The woman took it and thumbed it open, looking over it to make sure

Emma hadn't swapped it out. Her smile when she saw the paper was quick and cruel.

"Stay out of my way," she warned the group. "I see you again...I shoot first and talk never."

She turned and left, only putting the gun away when she was almost in sight of the building. Jacob sagged against the wall, and Emma hugged Max tight, making sure he was okay.

"That...wasn't fun," Max admitted. He sounded shaky, but otherwise okay.

"I can't believe she got the clue," Emma said. "Isn't there anything we can do to stop her? Call the police? Call the guards? We're in a fort, are there still guards?"

"We don't have to," Jacob said. He turned toward his girlfriend, and with surprise she saw that he was smiling.

"What do you mean?" Emma asked.

"I already read the paper," he reminded her. "And I know exactly where the final clue is."

Working on the Railway

Jacob called a cab to take them to the airport. Using the notes app on his phone, he recreated what he had seen on the paper before he handed it over. Then he turned it so the others could see. It was just three words: DIE ROOF HEARTLAND.

"That's it?" Emma asked. "That was the whole clue?"

"What if there was more but you could only see it under blacklights?" Max said.

"Luckily for us, they didn't have blacklights in the 1800s," his sister teasd him. "These three words must mean something."

"The heartland is what people call Middle America, isn't it?" Jacob asked.

"Yeah, but it seems like Galt was Canadian, since he hid his clues in Canada," Emma said. "The heartland could be Scotland, but in those days that would have been a trip that lasted months. I don't think he would have gone home just to hide a clue."

"Could it be where Levi is buried?" Max asked.

"Good guess," Jacob said, "but he wasn't dead when Galt made the clues. He was on the run from the police."

"Maybe it's an anagram?" Emma wondered.

"What's that?" Max asked.

"You know, when they mix all the letters up to make new words," she explained.

"Maybe!" Jacob started breaking the words up on his note app, trying to find different combinations. At the same time, Emma found a website online that would solve an anagram for her. But when she inserted the word, the website gave her *thousands* of different possibilities. Some of them made no sense at all. "HER ORA DEFLATION?" she read with a laugh. "HOT ALOE INFRARED?"

"Railroad," Jacob yelled, excited, holding out his work to show them. End of the railroad!" He punched the air in excitement.

"You did it!" Emma said, and gave him a kiss in celebration. Max pretended to be sick, and Emma laughed and gently punched his arm.

Jacob Googled 'end of the railroad in Canada 1862.' He found a ton of articles about the railroad and started to skim through them. "Let's see…the Last Spike was driven on the Canadian Pacific Railroad on 7 November, 1885 by Donald Smith… blah blah, Eagle Pass… blah blah… Aha! Today tourists can visit the Last Spike on the Trans-Canada Highway, forty-five kilometres west of Revelstoke. The site includes a seasonal gift shop, picnic area, and monument!"

"Are we really going to go to British Columbia?" Emma asked. "Your mom must be freaking out."

Jacob checked his phone. "Eight missed calls," he admitted. "And a whole bunch of angry, worried text messages." He ran a hand through his hair, thinking. "But that woman has the clue. And I don't think it'll take her very long to crack, either. We have to get there before she does…or all of this was for nothing."

All three teenagers slept on the eight-hour overnight flight across the country. They were exhausted from their long search, and from the danger they were in. Max dreamed of arriving at the site and wrestling the evil woman for her gun. He was a hero! Emma dreamed of a police chase through a dark city. She held the treasure in her hands, but when she looked down, she saw it was Max she was holding in her arms. Jacob dreamed of his father.

In the dream, his father was just a teenager himself. "It's a family legacy," he told Jacob. "You understand."

"But it's my birthday," Jacob said. He was holding a balloon that read '16' on it.

"Here. Happy birthday." His father handed Jacob a box.

Jacob unwrapped the box. It was a wooden chest with a puzzle lid. When Jacob opened the box...it was empty. He looked up, but his father was gone.

Getting to Revelstoke was easy, but getting from there to the site of the Last Spike was another thing. There were no tourist buses taking people to the site, and they couldn't rent a car because they were under 25.

"We could hitchhike," Jacob said.

"No way," Emma said. "I'm not getting into a stranger's car with Max. Besides, we might need to get away fast. We can't just hang out waiting for a lift and hoping that woman doesn't show up while we're there."

"Good point." Jacob sighed and rubbed his face. He was still exhausted. Sleeping on the plane hadn't exactly been comfortable, and he was feeling guilty about just how much he had spent on plane tickets. If they couldn't find this treasure, his mom was going to ground him forever. And he would have to pay back every penny, which would probably take him a whole summer of full-time work.

"How far did you say it was?" Emma asked. "Maybe we could walk."

Jacob typed the two places into his map app and groaned. "Forty-five minutes to drive…eleven hours to walk or bike!"

"Taxi?" Max suggested.

"What if they don't want to wait around while we find the clue?" Emma asked. "We'll be in the same position as if we hitchhiked."

"Lyft, maybe?" Jacob said. "We can negotiate with the driver before we leave for them to stick around and get the fare back. I bet it would be worth it, so they don't have to drive back with no fare."

"Good idea!" Emma brought up the ridesharing app and typed their destination in. She used the 'round trip' function to write the Revelstoke airport as their destination and drop-off point. A few minutes later, it dinged to announce that someone had accepted the ride. Emma called the driver, explained that they wanted to see the site and would be about half an hour, and negotiated an added tip to cover the extra wait time.

Fifteen minutes later, they were all getting into a big black truck. The driver was in his late sixties, with a huge salt-and-pepper beard and a smile that was almost as big.

"Welcome to Revelstoke!" he said. "Sightseeing today?"

"Yeah, we're just…huge fans of the railroad," Jacob said. The lie sounded bad even to him, and the driver definitely gave them a strange look.

"Where are your parents?" the man asked.

"At the hotel," Emma said. "They weren't interested in seeing the Last Spike, but they told us we could go on our own."

"You know it won't be cheap," the driver warned them. "There and back and the tip for the wait?"

"They're divorced," Jacob said. "We're here with Dad and his new girlfriend. We could ask for anything and he would say yes."

The driver laughed at that, a big laugh that shook his whole body. "Oh, yeah. I've been there. I'm on my third wife," he said, and turned the car on.

As they drove, the driver chatted with his passengers. Emma, Max, and Jacob were too tired to answer much, but he didn't seem to mind. He kept up the conversation for all of them. His name was Pete, was a retired oil patch worker. He had made a fortune over the years, he told them, but lost half of it every time he got divorced. He had left the North of B.C. to retire in Revelstoke, and he drove Lyft mostly for the company—and to get out of his wife's hair!

He talked about everything from the oil industry to his five kids to the effect of climate change on B.C. wildlife. He was especially worried about the mountain pine beetle. The lack of cold winters meant they weren't dying off, and they were destroying a lot of the trees. Revelstoke relied on forestry and tourism, so it was a big problem. It kept him busy for ten minutes, and then he was on to the next topic.

Finally, they reached the turn off for the Last Spike. Ted pulled into the parking lot. There were a few other cars there, but it wasn't too busy. "I'm just going to have a little nap," Ted told them. "You take your time. And be mindful of the tracks—there's a train coming back in a few minutes, and those things are killer."

"Thanks, Ted," Emma said.

They got out of the truck and looked around. The gift shop was a cute little red building with white trim, designed to look like an old-fashioned train station. There was even a line of track in front of it, just for show. A huge red train caboose sat off to one side, with signs inviting tourists to explore it. A chain-link fence separated the tourist attraction from the actual railway that Ted had warned them about. There was almost a huge stone cairn with a sign explaining what the Last Spike was.

The trio went over to the sign. It read, "The 100th Anniversary of the Driving of the Last Spike was Commemorated Here."

"This wasn't here when Galt left his clues," Emma said. "So what was?"

"That's what I'd like to know," a familiar voice said.

All three kids spun around.

"No!" Jacob said.

It was the woman. She had been standing behind the cairn—hiding? Waiting for them? Her gun was out, but she had it low to her side so that no one would be able to see her. Even if they could, there was no one outside with them. The other tourists were in the gift shop, and Ted was probably sleeping in his truck.

No one was coming to save them.

"Believe it or not, I'm glad you're here," the woman said. "I was worried you might not show up."

"Why would you want us here?" Emma asked.

"Because I can't find the damn clue," the woman snapped. "I've been here for three hours. The cairn was only built in 1985, so it can't be there. I checked the caboose and the gift shop. You had better figure it out. Or I'll start by shooting the kid." She pointed the gun at Max.

"You really are a monster," Jacob snapped. "You're just like Levi Boone Helm."

The woman laughed. "Helm? Oh, kid. I'm not related to Helm."

"But...you said this treasure was your birthright," Jacob said.

"It is." The woman drew up tall and proud. "My name is Melissa Galt. My ancestor was Frances Galt. He built all of these. Made these puzzles. Created this gift for Lucy Helm. And what did she do? She murdered him. She didn't want to share the money. It wasn't until Frances was dead that

Lucy realised they were supposed to work together to find the clues. She died young. Before she could even solve the puzzle box. But not before she got married, and gave birth to her son...Richard Melville."

Jacob stared at her. "What did you say?"

"That's right." Melissa grinned. "*You're* the descendant of the murder and the cannibal. *Your* ancestor was Levi Boone Helm."

The End of the Line

Jacob stared at Melissa. "No—that can't be true!" He couldn't believe that his ancestor had been the monster he had read about. Just hearing about the awful things Levi Boone Helm had done had made Jacob feel sick. Did he really have that DNA in him? Could it be true?

"Why did you think your father was obsessed with this treasure?" Melissa asked. "I came to him and told him about the puzzle box. He went looking for it, and found it in an old family heirloom. But when I offered to buy it from him, he wanted to work together." Melissa's lip curled and she spat on the ground. "He thought that I should *split* the fortune with him. That since it had been Helm's he was *owed*. As if Lucy Helm hadn't murdered Frances! As if he didn't owe *me* for everything that was taken from my family! Idiot. I didn't want to kill him, but he left me no choice. He wouldn't sell the puzzle box."

"He was going to split it?" Emma asked. There were tears in her eyes. "And you still killed him?"

"It's my treasure," the woman snarled. She sounded deranged, and Jacob took a step back from her. "Now you have the same choice! Tell me where the clue is—or you die." She lifted the gun up.

Jacob held his hands out. "Okay, okay. Let me think. Just...let me think."

He looked around. Melissa said she had already searched the area. Was there anything she might have missed? She had been looking at man-made things. The caboose, the monument, the gift shop. But none of that had been there when Frances Galt left his hidden message.

Frances Galt…

No.

"Do you have the letter?" he asked Melissa. "The one from Levi to Lucy?"

Melissa looked at him, suspicious, but then nodded. Keeping back, and with her gun still out, she took off her backpack and pulled out the unlocked puzzle box. She took out the first letter, laid it on the ground, and then backed away. With the gun, she motioned for Jacob to take the letter.

He picked it up and read it over. "In the letter, Levi says that Galt is leaving three clues. The leaves at the Library of Parliament are one. The stones in the Citadel in Halifax are the second…"

"And the third is here, at the railway," Melissa said.

Jacob nodded. "And the only thing that was here when Galt was here, was…the railway itself. That's where the clue is. Carved into the railway itself."

They all turned to look.

The railway was just beyond a chain-link fence. There was a bend not too far away, and grass was growing up between the tracks.

"Let me go," Jacob insisted. "I can find the clue, and I promise that I'll tell you what it actually says.

"Are you insane?" Emma asked. "It's way too dangerous! That's an active train line."

"I can do it. You have to let me do it," Jacob said. He started to move toward the fence.

"No way!" Melissa said, bringing her gun up. "You're way too determined to go yourself. What's your plan, huh? Lie to me about the clue you find? Send me on a wild goose chase so that you have time to find the real clue?"

"No!" Jacob said. "I just…uh… I wanted to…"

Melissa snorted. "I thought so. Stay right where you are. I'm going over. And don't think about making a run for it—I've got great aim, and there's nowhere to hide."

"You can't—there's a train on the way!" Emma said.

"I'm not falling for that," Melissa said. She walked over to the fence, checked to make sure that no one was coming, and started to climb. Every few feet she waved the gun at the kids, to make sure they stayed where they were.

Jacob put an arm around Emma and held her close. "When the train comes," he whispered, "she'll be distracted coming back over, and we can make a run for it."

Emma nodded, relieved. "What about the clue?" she whispered back. "She'll go back for it as soon as the train passes."

Jacob tried to hide his smile, in case Melissa was watching. "I don't think the clue is there at all," he whispered back.

Melissa dropped to the other side of the fence. She turned again, to make sure the kids were still standing still. She looked around, then crossed over the tracks so that she could look at them and keep the kids in her sight-line at the same time.

"I don't think that's a good idea!" Emma called out. "You should stay on this side so you can get out faster!"

"And turn my back on you? I wasn't born yesterday," Melissa called back. She kept her gun pointed at them, and turned her attention to the tracks.

Jacob nervously looked down the tracks. Because of the bend, he couldn't see if a train was on the way. Pete had said it would be here any minute...but what if it didn't come in time? What if Melissa got angry that she couldn't find a clue, and decided to start shooting?

"Jacob," Emma whispered. "is that—?" She held a hand up, like she was listening.

Jacob stopped breathing. He thought, in the distance, he might hear something like the rumble of a train. But with the highway so close by, it was hard to tell what was just traffic and what might be a train.

"Melissa!" he yelled. "I think that's a train! You need to cross back over!"

"Shut up!" she yelled back. "I think I see some marks on this tie, but it might just be worn. I can't tell!" She crouched down to get a better look.

"Melissa!" Emma screamed. "It's the train! It's the train!"

Melissa stood up, so that she was standing directly in the centre of the tracks. "Do you think I'm an idiot?" she yelled. "I'm descended from Frances Galt! He was a genius, who hid puzzles in plain sight for centuries! You think I'm going to be tricked by a bunch of stupid—"

The train whistle was deafening. As it came around the corner, Melissa turned halfway toward it. Emma grabbed Max and turned him away, and just in time. The train was moving so fast it almost seemed to appear out of thin air. One second there was Melissa, and then there was a blur...and the long, long line of the rain, and blood on the tracks.

The screech of the train's brakes filled the air. Jacob grabbed Emma's arm, and the two of them hurried Max away. Emma and Max were both crying, and Jacob couldn't stop his hands from shaking.

"She wouldn't listen," Emma said. "I told her, I told her..."

"It wasn't your fault," Jacob said. "I told her that's where the clue was. I lied..."

"You thought she would run when the train came," Emma said. "I did, too. We told her. There was time!"

Jacob hugged her, and Max too, and they all took a moment to catch their breath. The train was still trying to brake, and the long line of its boxes was starting to slow down. They all avoided looking at the track, and what was left of Melissa's body.

"What did you mean—you lied about where the clue was?" Max asked, sniffling and wiping his nose on his sleeve.

"The third puzzle wasn't the train tracks," Jacob explained. "It was the puzzle box. It was curling—that means Galt made it, not Levi."

"But that means…" Emma said. "That means Levi left the clue here?"

Jacob nodded. "And Levi was here in 1862. That was before they drove in the Last Spike—four years before. Galt must have used the Last Spike as his clue in the Halifax puzzle because it had been finished by the time he was done hiding clues. That means the clue isn't tied to the railway at all. It's something simple. Levi wasn't a genius. He was just a murderer."

"He would have hidden it somewhere simple. Somewhere natural," Emma said.

They all looked around. There was a little area around the gift shop with rocks and lawn, but just past that there was forest. And right at the edge of the forest...

"Is that a cave?" Jacob asked.

People from the gift shop were starting to come outside to see why the train had stopped. It wouldn't be long before they noticed Melissa's body. Jacob ran over to the cave, and Emma and Max followed right before.

It was barely a cave, just a little area where the rock had been worn away over time. No one would ever think twice about it.

And in the cave, carved into the rock wall by the edge of a knife, were a few simple words.

"My words have the answer," Max read. "Then he's written 4, 6, 2."

"My words?" Emma asked.

"It can't be...can it?" Jacob reached into his pocket and took out the letter that Melissa had given him to reread. "Could the location of the treasure have been hidden in the note all along?"

He spread the paper out on the ground, and the trio crowded around. The letter read:

Lucy, you were five when I left you, and you are so grown up now.

We have so much in common, two of us with each other. You may not know

what for was the reason I left you, but life is hard to understand. I've found

a fortune in five and thirty gold nuggets, and left it with other treasures I've

collected in my travels. In three days or three years, the police will come for

me. None of them will catch me. But if they do, and they hang me,

Galt will go north and hide clues that will point you to the treasure. When

you are ready to be one who is rich, he will bring you the first clue. Only

you two working together will be able to solve the clues. Work with him

together, for you alone will not find the answers. Lucy, I am sorry that I was

not a better father, us two together were good, but I could not find no

love, theree in my heart for your mother. You know she is not a kind

woman, she went for me because I was fun but then the fun

ran out and she wanted nòne more of what I had to give.

No, nòne of her love was left for me. So I gave all of mine to you.

Find the treasure west of here, Lucy, and know that I love you.

And use it when you find it to make your life better.

Give the kind of life to yourself I never could give to you, do not

work like a dog, for people who love you not, no, instead

build a fire from the wood of their expectations and thrive.

Dad.

"What were the numbers on the wall?" Jacob asked.

"4, 6, 2," Max read out. Emma handed Jacob a pen, and he carefully circled the fourth word in the first line, the sixth word in the second line, and the second word in the third line. He kept up that pattern for the whole book, until the letter read:

Lucy, you were **five** when I left you, and you are so grown up now.

We have so much in common, **two** of us with each other. You may not know

what **for** was the reason I left you, but life is hard to understand. I've found

a fortune in **five** and thirty gold nuggets, and left it with other treasures I've

collected in my travels. In **three** days or three years, the police will come for

me. **None** of them will catch me. But if they do, and they hang me,

Galt will go **north** and hide clues that will point you to the treasure. When

you are ready to be **one** who is rich, he will bring you the first clue. Only

you **two** working together will be able to solve the clues. Work with him

together, for you **alone** will not find the answers. Lucy, I am sorry that I was

not a better father, us **two** together
were good, but I could not find no

love, **theree** in my heart for your
mother. You know she is not a kind

woman, she went **for** me because I
was fun but then the fun

ran out and she wanted **nòne** more of
what I had to give.

No, **nòne** of her love was left for me. So
I gave all of mine to you.

Find the treasure **west of** here, Lucy,
and know that I love you.

And use it when you **find** it to make
your life better.

Give **the** kind of life to yourself I never
could give to you, do not

work like a **dog**, for people who love
you not, no, instead

build a fire from the **wood** of their
expectations and thrive.

Dad.

"It's a bunch of numbers!" Emma said, excitedly copying down the words. 245302, then north, then 12123400, then West."

"And then it says find the dogwood!" Max said.

"I think those zeros might be nines," Jacob said. "See the weird little dots above the O? Nine is a hard word to sneak into a letter, and he uses none in weird ways."

"Let me check." Emma divided the numbers up into longitude and latitude: 52°45'39.2"N 121°23'49.9"W and 52°45'30.2"N 121°23'40.0"W. She put them both into Google Maps and checked to see where they were. They were both in BC, but with 0s, the number landed in the middle of a lake. With the 9s, it was near where Levi

Boone Helm had been captured. "This is it!" Emma said, excited. "This is where the treasure is!"

The Lost Treasure

Jacob, Emma, and Max went back to the car. Pete was awake, and watching the train. It had stopped, and there were a lot of people gathered around.

"Kids!" Pete gasped. "Oh thank God. There was an accident on the tracks—I thought one of you might have been hurt!!"

"There was an accident?" Jacob asked. "Did anyone get hurt?"

Pete looked over at the train, and then at Max. "I'm not sure," he lied, "but I think it's best we get you back to your hotel right away. I bet your dad will be worried sick."

Emma thanked him, and they all got into the truck. It was a quiet ride back to Revelstoke. The kids were shaken by what had happened to Melissa, but they were also excited about being so close to the treasure.

It wouldn't be long before they found the famous treasure... Would it be worth it? None of them were sure.

They gave Pete the address for the hotel closest to the airport, and as soon as he had pulled away they started walking.

But they weren't expecting what happened when they walked inside...

"Mom!?" Jacob gasped.

His mother was at the information counter in the tiny airport, arguing with someone on the phone. When she heard Jacob's voice she spun around.

"Jacob!" she screamed. She was across the airport in seconds and hugging her son close. When he felt her arms go around him, the stress of the last few days hit him hard. He found himself blinking away tears.

"Mom! How did you find us?" he asked.

"I get the credit card statements, you idiot!" she said. "What the hell were you thinking? Running off after some treasure when someone with a *gun* was chasing you! I've been worried sick! And Emma!" She turned on her son's girlfriend. "I thought you would talk some sense into him! How could you bring Max into this?"

"Mom," Jacob said, but Emma cut him off.

"I thought it was safer to bring him with us," Emma said. She felt so embarrassed. At the time it had made a lot of sense, but now? Standing in front of Jacob's very angry mother? She wasn't sure it had been a good idea at all.

"A woman with a *gun!*" Jacob's mom said again.

"Mom!" Jacob said again.

"What?!" his mother yelled.

"We did it. We found the lost treasure. What Dad spent his life looking for…what he died for…we found it."

It took a lot of explaining, but Jacob and Emma laid out everything that had happened since the break-in in Toronto. Jacob's mom interrupted constantly with questions, asking why they had done certain things, why not others, and often, "Just what were you thinking?!" When they told her what happened with Melissa at the end, Emma cried again, and Jacob's mom held her tight until she was done. Jacob hugged Max close, too, and they all took a moment before they kept going.

But by the end, as she held the final clue in her hand, Jacob could tell that his mother was curious.

"Please, Mom," he said. "I can't leave it like this. I know my dad wasn't a good husband. He wasn't a good dad, either. This treasure hunt he was on...it wasn't the reason he was always gone. He only started looking for it when Melissa told him about the box. He was obsessed with treasure. I know. But I know...if we can find the treasure...I can find a way to say goodbye.... And pay off your credit card for all those flights," he added hopefully.

"Kid, you are going to be paying back every penny of those flights from your own money," his mom said. "You are in the kind of trouble most kids only dream about! You made a lot of bad decisions this week, and I'm not going to let that go. You hear me? You are grounded. For a year." She stopped and looked over at Emma and Max, and then back to Jacob. "As soon as we get back from digging up that treasure," she added.

Jacob laughed. "Are you serious? Do you mean it?" he gasped.

"Let's go rent a car," his mother said.

It turned out it was almost an eight-hour drive, so they got the next flight to Williams Lake and rented a car from there, instead. From there it was only a two-hour drive out to Cariboo. The nearby Keithley Creek was a ghost town now, with no sign of even the buildings that used to be there, but there was a road that went most of the way to their destination. After that, they had to go down some old logging roads. Luckily, the 4x4 that Jacob's mother had rented could handle it.

From there, it was a little bit of a hike through beautiful old-growth forests. Emma kept an eye on Max, reminding him to drink water, and Jacob and his mom carried the heavy shovels they had bought in Williams Lake. Most of the trees around them were fir, spruce, cedar and hemlock. But as they arrived near the location, Max saw the bright white of a dogwood flower.

"There!" he yelled.

"Hold on… there's more than one!" Jacob said. "What do we do?"

They dropped their supplies and explored the area. There were dogwood trees here and there, and they looked out of place in the forest. They counted seventeen in total.

"How do we know which it is?" Emma asked.

"He probably planted one, and the others spread from it. We need to find the largest," Jacob's mom suggested.

They spread out again, and eventually agreed on what they thought was the biggest tree. Jacob and his mom got out their shovels and started to dig. It wasn't long before Jacob's shovel clanged against metal. "Here!" he yelled. "I found something!"

His mom joined him, and soon they had a big hole. And in the centre was an old metal steamer trunk. Jacob knocked off the old, rusted lock easily with the shovel. He opened the top of the trunk...

And found a huge pile of gold nuggets, watches, jewellery, and other stolen treasures. It was a fortune...and since it was his family inheritance, it was completely legal to dig it up and keep it.

They all took turns touching the gold, picking up necklaces, and running coins through their fingers.

"Wow," Emma said. "I can't believe it. We really did it. We really found the treasure."

Jacob sat back, wiping a hand across his forehead. He couldn't believe it. He had done what his dad set out to do. He picked up a piece of gold and looked up at the sky.

"This is for you, Dad," he thought. *"I love you.*

Emma sat down next to him as his mom and her brother figured out how to divide the treasure up so that they could carry it home.

"Are you okay?" she asked. "Does it feel like saying goodbye to your dad?"

"I'm okay," he said. "I know this whole thing was scary and messaged but. But... It was kind of awesome, too. Getting to finish what he started. Getting to see what treasure hunting is really like."

"You know..." Emma said. "There are other famous Canadian treasures that no one has been able to find. And we made a pretty good team."

Jacob laughed. "I think I've had enough treasure hunting. For now, at least, I'd like to focus on graduating high school...and on doing this."

He kissed her. Laughing, she kissed him back.

"Okay," she agreed, "that sounds fun, too."

THE END

Table des matières

9 782490 586523